That stops them in their tracks . . .

"We might find **GOLD**
or something **OLD!**

We love to go **EXPLORING!**"

The path is blocked —
a **PILE** *of* **ROCKS!**

How will they travel through it?

"You **ROLL**, I'll **MOW** – and off we go!"

But then a **WALL**
so wide and tall!

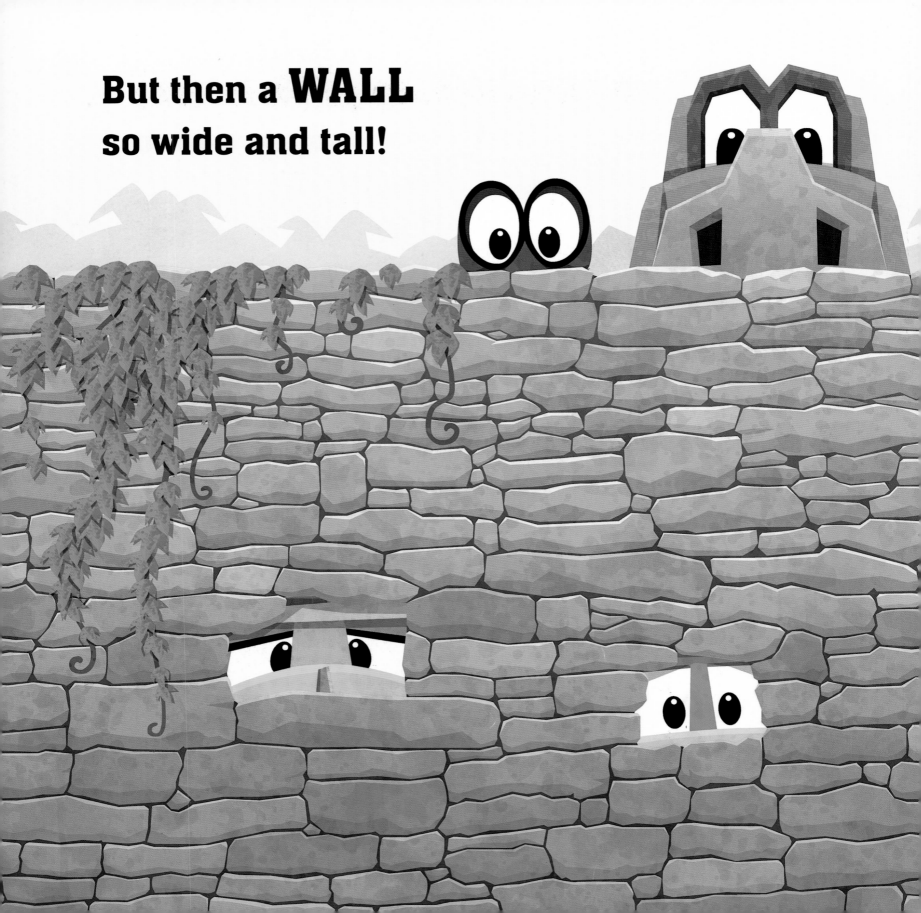

"I can DRILL beneath this hill, WHIRRRRRRRRRRRRRRRR!!!

DRILLERSAURUS 9

we'll get through in no time!"

At last they reach
a sandy beach.
Suddenly,
a sound . . .

What's that BUZZ?

What's this?

"My tail because . . . there's metal underground!"

"A submarine?
I'll **SWEEP** it clean . . ."

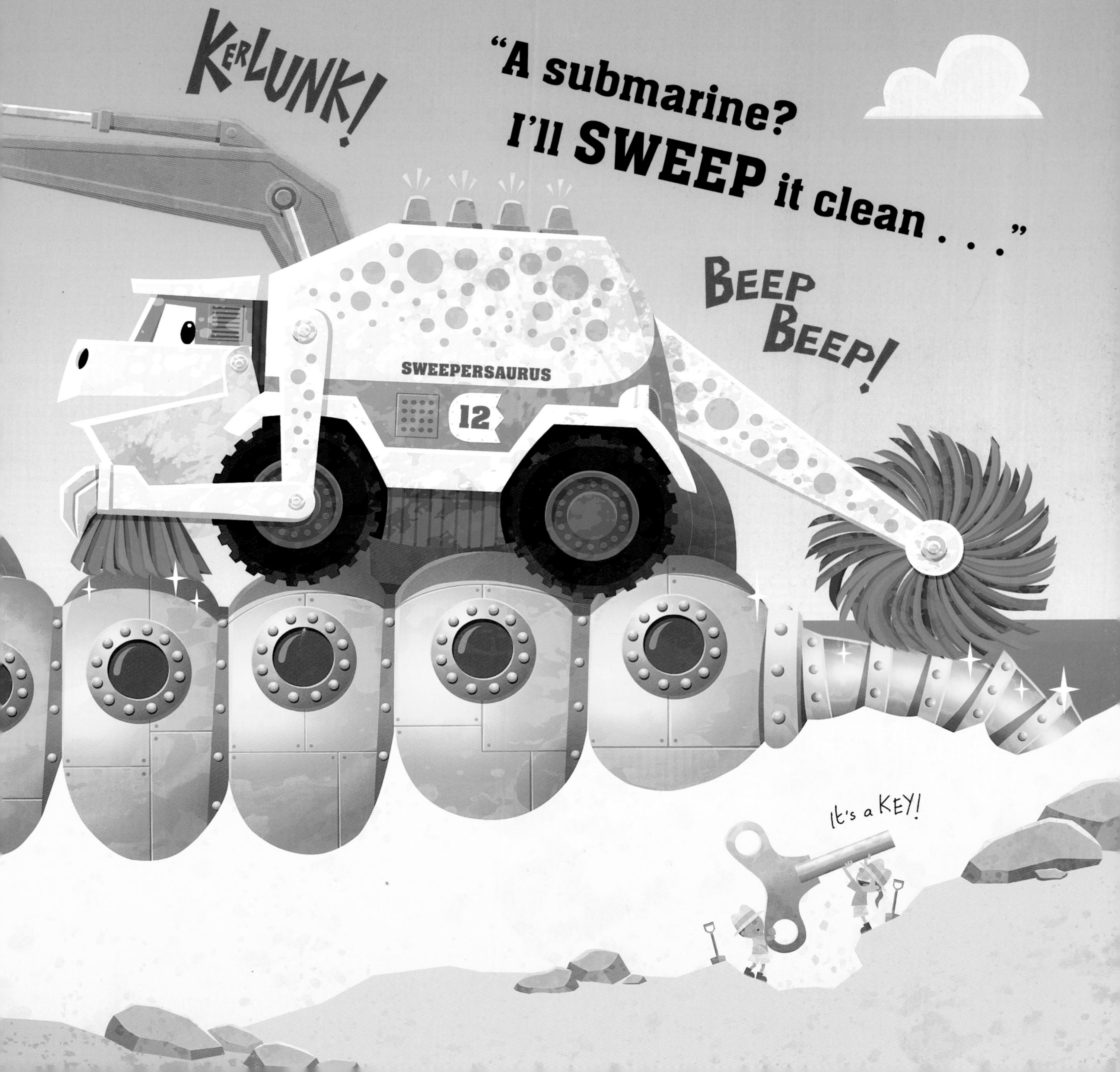

And he roars — "Thanks, **DIGGERSAURS**,
I've been stuck here
for years!

I've missed the sea,
but now I'm free!
Please help me shift my gears."

"We did find **GOLD**
and something **OLD** –

THE **GIANT** DIVERSAURUS!"

TREASURE!!!

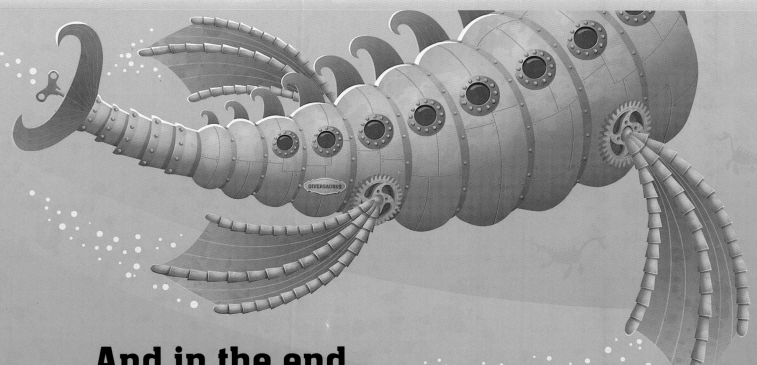

**And in the end
a newfound friend
for DIGGERSAUR EXPLORERS!**

For Gillian

Explore this book and find these treasures!

PUFFIN BOOKS

UK | USA | Canada | Ireland | Australia
India | New Zealand | South Africa

Puffin Books is part of the Penguin Random House group of companies
whose addresses can be found at global.penguinrandomhouse.com.

www.penguin.co.uk   www.puffin.co.uk   www.ladybird.co.uk

First published 2018
001

Copyright © Michael Whaite, 2018
The moral right of the author has been asserted

Printed in China
A CIP catalogue record for this book is available from the British Library

ISBN: 978-0-141-37551-9

All correspondence to:
Puffin Books, Penguin Random House Children's, 80 Strand, London WC2R ORL